Mademoiselle Gorilla

Written by
SIMON PUTTOCK

Illustrated by
NICOLA SLATER

MACMILLAN
CHILDREN'S BOOKS

Mademoiselle Gorilla lived in the forest with her mother and father and three aunts and four uncles and five cousins.

Her family loved to whoop and tumble, and eat bananas, and snore and grunt in their sleep.

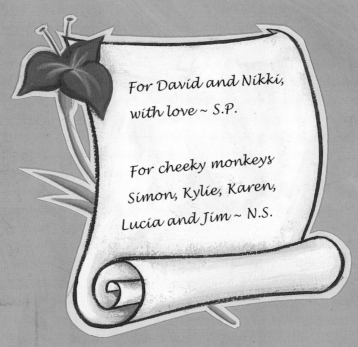

For David and Nikki,
with love ~ S.P.

For cheeky monkeys
Simon, Kylie, Karen,
Lucia and Jim ~ N.S.

First published in 2004 by Macmillan Children's Books
A division of Macmillan Publishers Limited
20 New Wharf Road, London N1 9RR
Basingstoke and Oxford
Associated companies throughout the world
www.panmacmillan.com

ISBN 1 4050 2034 2

A CIP catalogue record for this book is available from the British Library.
Printed in Belgium by Proost.

But Mademoiselle Gorilla was different.

"I do not grunt or snore.
I do not tumble or whoop," she said.
"I am a sensitive soul.
I have written a poem –

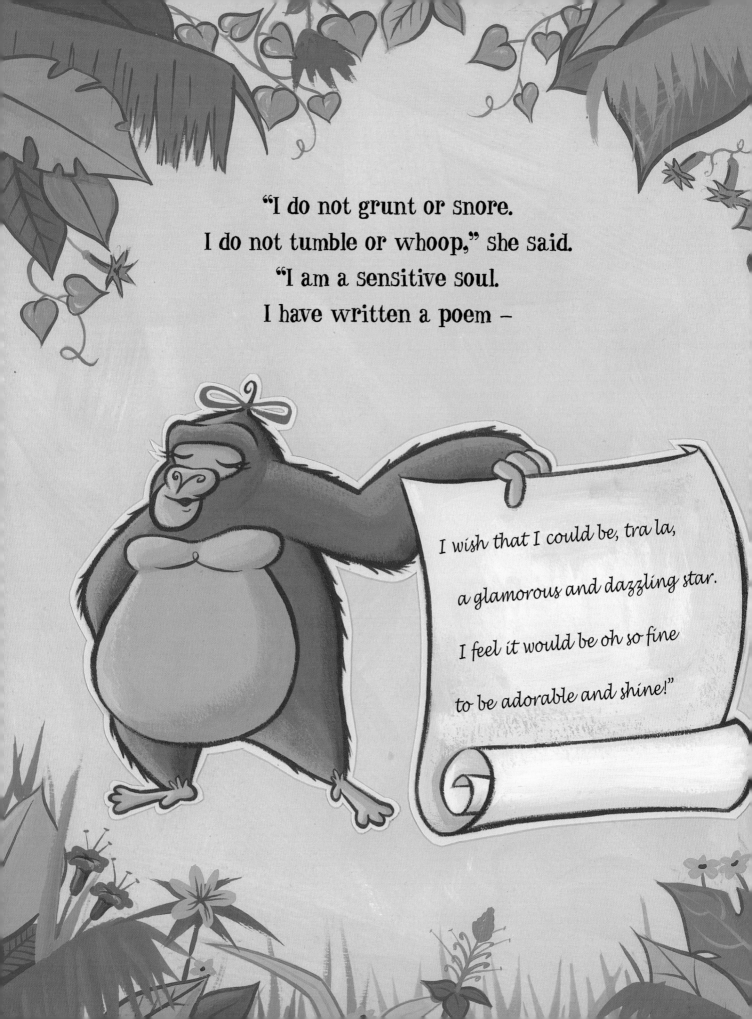

I wish that I could be, tra la,

a glamorous and dazzling star.

I feel it would be oh so fine

to be adorable and shine!"

Ho Ho!

"HOO HOO!" her family laughed. "That's so funny! Gorillas are hairy, not shiny. Hoo hoo!"

Hoo Hoo!

Hee Hee!

"But it is not meant to be funny, it is a poem,"

Ho Ho!

said Mademoiselle Gorilla crossly. "YOU are typical apes. I am a poet. And since I am not appreciated here, I will go somewhere where I shall be."

So Mademoiselle Gorilla
made herself a dress of
leaves and caught the
boat to America.

The African Princess

In New York, Mademoiselle Gorilla recited her poem at smart parties.

She was a **great** success.

Everyone
shouted, "BRAVO!"
And, "What a charming dress!"
Soon, all the posh ladies were
wearing leafy dresses too!
And Mademoiselle Gorilla felt appreciated

At one **very** smart party,
Mademoiselle Gorilla
was spotted by a famous
Hollywood film director.

"You are **adorable**,"
he said, "and I can
make you a star.
You **must** be in
my next film."

It was
another chance
to shine.
Mademoiselle
Gorilla said,
"Yes please."

So, bright and early
next morning,

she hopped

on a plane

to Hollywood.

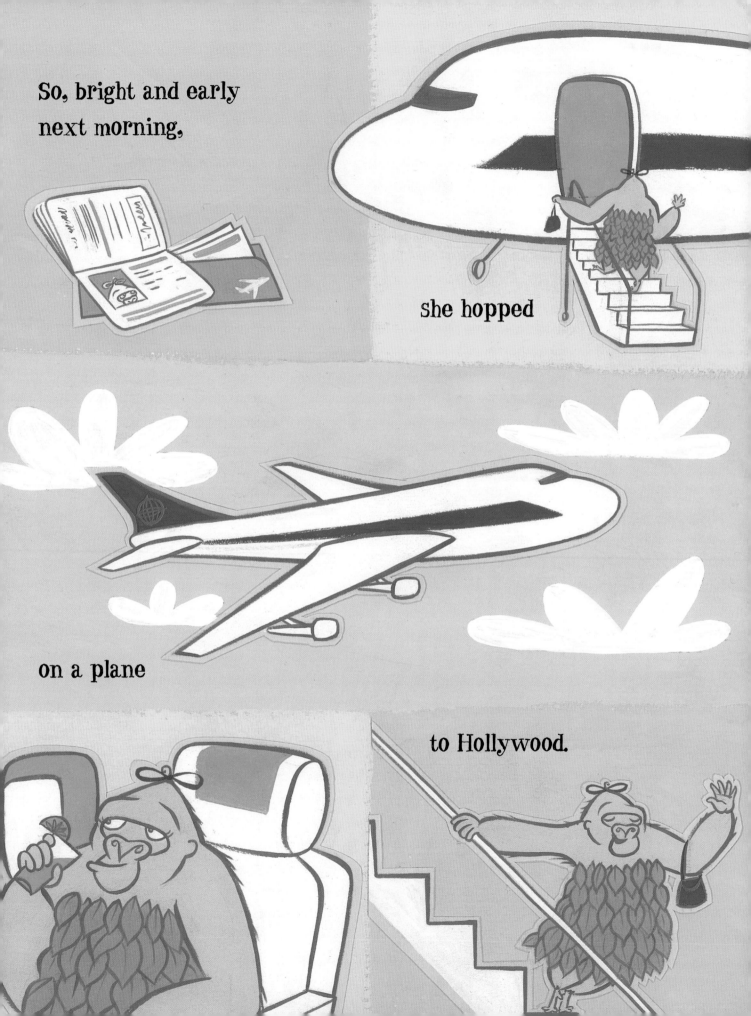

"My dear," said the famous director, "please be a typical ape. Feel free to whoop and tumble, and eat bananas, and snore and grunt in your sleep."

"Well," said Mademoiselle Gorilla,
"I am **not** a typical ape,
I am really a poet, you know . . .

but I will do it, just this once."

When the film was finished, there was a glittery party.

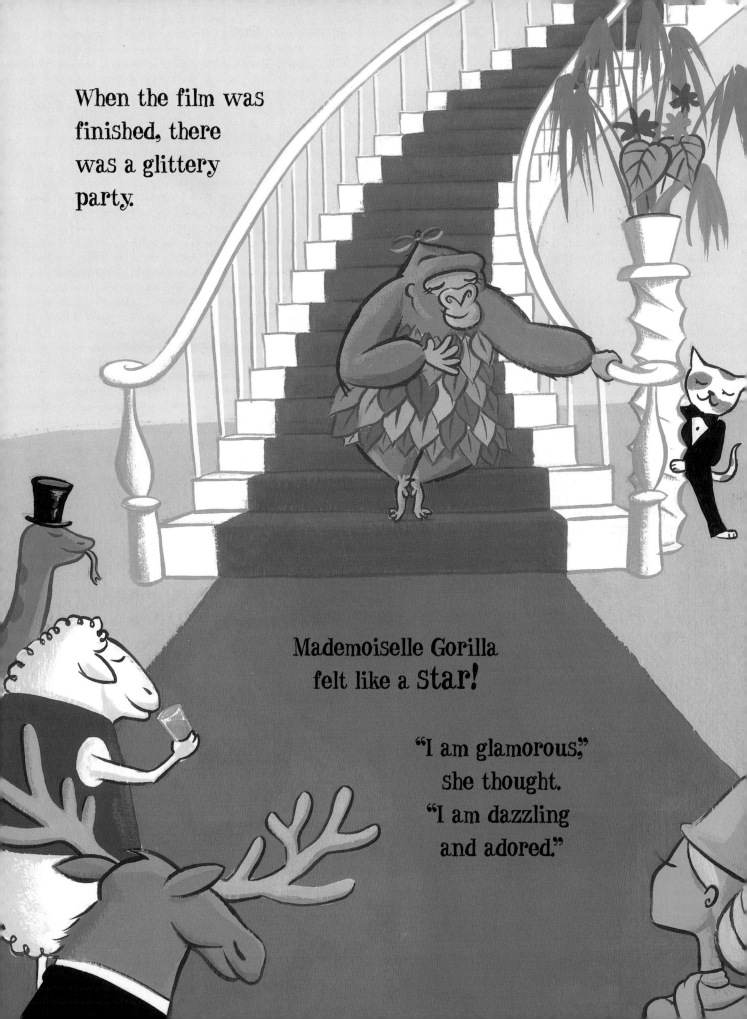

Mademoiselle Gorilla felt like a star!

"I am glamorous," she thought. "I am dazzling and adored."

But . . .

when Mademoiselle Gorilla saw herself on the silver screen, being a **typical** ape, she thought longingly of the forest ... and her family ...

and she began to feel TERRIBLY homesick,

The famous director, however, was delighted. "I am a hit!" he cried.

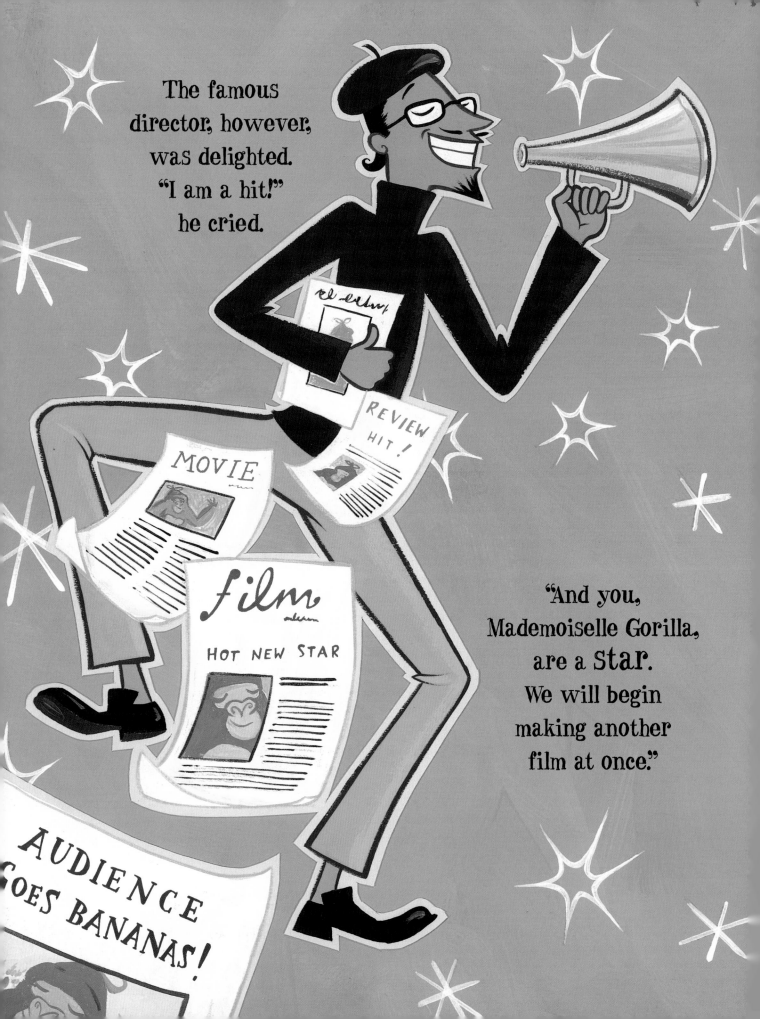

MOVIE

REVIEW HIT!

film

HOT NEW STAR

AUDIENCE GOES BANANAS!

"And you, Mademoiselle Gorilla, are a star. We will begin making another film at once."

To everyone's astonishment,
Mademoiselle Gorilla said, "No thank you."
"Nonsense!" cried the famous director.
"I can make you rich as well as a star."

"Thank you again," said Mademoiselle,

"but no. Poets are seldom rich,
and gorillas, never.

It
is
time
for me
to go home."

Mademoiselle Gorilla's family were **ever** so pleased to have her back.

They did not know that she was now a famous poet and movie star. She was simply their very own Mademoiselle, and she had come home.

"Was it nice in America?" asked Mademoiselle Gorilla's mother.
"It was fabulous," said Mademoiselle, "but I did miss you all.
And I have written another poem – listen ...

"HOO HOO!"
her family laughed.
"You're being funny again.
We do adore you."

And Mademoiselle Gorilla
was happy, because now
she knew that her family
all appreciated her in their
own special, gorillary way.

"You know what," she said.
"East or west, home's always best,
because I love you too.
And tonight I'm going to whoop it up,
because sometimes, that's what gorillas do."